This book belongs to:

....

....

Quarto is the authority on a wide range of topics.

Quarto educates, entertains and enriches the lives of our readers—enthusiasts and lovers of hands-on living.

www.quartoknows.com

Editor: Carly Madden
Designer: Victoria Kimonidou
Editorial Director: Victoria Garrard
Art Director: Laura Roberts-Jensen
Associate Publisher: Maxime Boucknooghe
Publisher: Zeta Jones

A CIP record for this book is
available from the Library of Congress.

ISBN 978 1 60992 938 1

Printed in China

THE EXTREMELY GREEDY
DRAGON

Jessica Barrah

Illustrated by Chris Saunders

The village of Little Chiddling had a big problem.
A big, scaly, fire-breathing problem.

A sleeping dragon on a railway line!

People tried to wake him up,
but the dragon kept Snoring.

"There'll be a reward!" announced the mayor.
"For anyone who can move the dragon off the tracks."

"I'd like a reward!" said Georgie Johnson.
"I need a new bike. I'll move the dragon!"

Nobody noticed the tiny girl riding up to the **huge** dragon.

The dragon might be
hungry, thought Georgie.

"Wake up!" she said, rustling
a bag of potato chips.

The dragon's nostrils quivered, and his eyelids fluttered.

SNAP!

He gobbled up the chips.

"Do you have any more food?" asked the dragon.

"I'm sure we can find some," said Georgie. "Follow me!"

In the park, the villagers gazed gloomily at the wet grass and damp picnic.

"Do you have any spare sandwiches?" asked the dragon.

"Cheese," said the parents, trembling. "And here's some cake."

"Yummy," said the dragon, as he breathed hot air over the grass.

Soon the grass was dry, but the dragon wanted **more** food.

Nearby, the village barbecue
fizzled with smoke.

"Can you help?" asked Georgie.
"Of course," said the dragon.

"Wonderful, thank you!"
said the cook, as the barbecue sizzled.

"Don't mention it," mumbled the
dragon, gobbling sausages.

"Still hungry?" asked Georgie.

Nearby, a wedding was in full swing.

"And finally, I'd like to say..." said the groom, "Dragon!"

"Is there any spare food for a greedy dragon?" asked Georgie.

"Help yourself!" said the groom, quivering.

The bride was **shivering**, so the dragon breathed out hot air to warm up the tent.

At the village festival, the mayor was worried.

"The festival fireworks are damp and a dragon's on the loose!" said the mayor.

"Where's Georgie?" shouted Georgie's mom.

"Behind you!"
cried Georgie.

"Don't worry!" laughed Georgie.
"The dragon's very friendly —
just a little greedy!"

"Friendly? Are you sure?"
said the mayor, suspiciously.

"He dried our wet park," said the parents.

"He lit our barbecue," added the cook.

"He warmed up our wedding!" said the bride.

"Well!" said the surprised mayor. "Would you like to stay? A handy dragon would be great for the village!"

"Ympph," nodded the dragon, through a mouthful of cotton candy.

"Was that a yes, greedy? You must start eating healthier food," scolded Georgie.

"Yes, you're right. I'll start tomorrow," promised the dragon, looking hopefully at a donut stall.

"Hooray!" shouted the crowd, as the dragon set off the festival fireworks.

Next Steps

Show the children the cover again. Could they have guessed what the story is about from looking at the cover?

Georgie was brave to try and move the dragon. The other people in the village were scared of the dragon. Why were they so scared? Are there things that scare the children? Can they remember a time when they were brave?

Ask the children if they've ever been surprised when somebody turns out to be different than expected.

The dragon is very helpful. What helpful things does the dragon do? Are the children helpful at home, or at school? Discuss what it feels like when someone helps you.

The dragon is extremely greedy. Are the children ever greedy? What happens if they eat too much food? What types of foods are healthy?

What do the children think a dragon would look like? Ask the children to draw a dragon eating their favorite food!